Babe and Friends™
The Complete Scrapbook

By Kenneth LaFreniere

Based on the motion picture screenplays:
<u>BABE: A Little Pig Goes a Long Way</u> written by George Miller & Chris Noonan
based on the book by Dick King-Smith
and <u>BABE: Pig in the City</u> written by George Miller Judy Morris Mark Lamprell
based on characters created by Dick King-Smith

Random House 🏠 New York

Library of Congress Catalog Card Number: 98-66575
www.randomhouse.com/kids
ISBN: 0-679-89386-5

Printed in the United States of America 10 9 8 7 6 5 4 3 2 1

Hi there. I'm Babe. And let me first say, "Welcome to my scrapbook!" It's really nice to have you here! I'm going to show you my favorite pictures from my most favorite adventures. I like all of these pictures a lot, and I hope you will, too!

This is the earliest picture of me. I think it's funny because I'm hanging upside down. Whoa!

This is me at the fair, looking at all the people having fun. I couldn't wait for one of them to take me home. And, luckily for me, the Boss brought me back to his wonderful farm.

That's the Boss. He's a real nice man.

The best thing about living on the Boss's farm is being with all of my friends.

That's the Boss and his wife, Mrs. Hoggett. I think they like it here almost as much as I do!

That's Rex and Fly, the sheepdogs. They help the Boss gather all the sheep together into a big flock. The sheep don't like Rex and Fly too much, because they can get a little rough sometimes. But I like them a whole lot.

Fly is like the mom I never had. I was taken from my real mom when I was very young. So Fly lets me call her "Mom," and that makes me happy. I think it makes her happy, too!

See, this is how happy Fly makes me.

This is my friend
Ferdinand. He's a duck who
thinks he's a rooster! He
always makes me laugh,
but sometimes he gets me
into trouble.

I don't know why he wanted me to take
the Boss's alarm clock, but you can see what
happened...

Who ever saw a blue pig before?

Not Rex, that's for sure! Most of the animals laughed and said they thought I looked funny. But Rex said that I couldn't play with Ferdinand anymore.

That made me sad.

BUT I couldn't stay that way for long. Even though Rex told me not to leave the pigsty, I couldn't help but play with everyone else. We have so much fun together!

See, I can't help it! Fly is so great, I just have to let her know how I feel!

That's me and another of my friends, Maa. A lot of people think sheep aren't smart, but it's not true. You just have to know how to talk to them.

Maa showed me how to talk to sheep. I think she's terrific!

And you know what? I think she feels the same way about me! She told her friends I was a nice pig. Isn't that something?

I get so happy that sometimes I just have to sing. La-la-la!

Sometimes I like to roam around and look for pretty things.

And sometimes I just like looking at people like you, because you're a pretty thing, too!

One day Fly and I noticed something strange happening in the field.

So did the sheep.

The Boss was building an obstacle course just like the one that's at the annual sheep-dog contest! And because Rex was sick and Fly was hurt, he wanted <u>me</u> to enter the contest—a contest for sheepdogs!

I'd always loved watching Fly and Rex help the Boss, and now I was going to have a chance to do it, too! I figured if I spoke very nicely, just the way Maa had taught me, the sheep would listen.

And look what happened

Since I turned out to be a good sheep-pig, the Boss entered me in the contest. The Boss is very fair—as long as I did the work well, he didn't care what kind of animal I was.

When I first walked out on the field, everyone laughed. They must have thought I looked pretty silly.

BUt when I led the sheep straight through the entire course, the crowd went wild!

Even though they had both wanted to be in the contest, Rex and Fly were happy that the Boss and I had done well.

After we got a perfect score and won the contest, the Boss looked down at me and said, "That'll do, Pig."

I was never so happy in my life!

I couldn't wait for my next adventure. And as luck would have it, I didn't have to wait long.

When we got back to the farm, I couldn't believe what was happening. Everyone was cheering—for me!

It made me feel pretty special.

Everyone was saying that I had done the farm proud.

They were <u>really</u> nice to me.

But then I did something dumb.

I got in the Boss's way, and he took a nasty fall. Now he couldn't get out of bed and it was all my fault!

I felt like the crummiest animal on the farm.

The Boss's wife did her best, but nothing was getting done the way it used to.

Pretty soon, these scary humans came to take the farm away.

They were from the Bank!

The Boss's wife figured out that the only way to save the farm was to take me to the state fair to earn some money. BUT that meant leaving the farm.

I didn't want to do that.

I'd miss all of my friends. Especially Fly.

Ferdinand didn't want me to go, either.

I mean, he <u>really</u> didn't want me to go.

BUT if that was the only way to save the farm, I knew I had to do it.

It was hard to say good-bye.

It was so hard for Ferdinand that he refused to do it! Can you believe that he tried to follow me and the Boss's wife all the way to the fair?

Unfortunately, the trip didn't go smoothly. When we reached the Big City, the airport police thought that the Boss's wife had done something bad!

They held her for a long time, and we missed our connecting flight.

Now we were stuck in the Big City.

I'd never seen so many humans running around so fast. And so many big buildings and loud cars. We definitely were not on the farm anymore!

Luckily, we found a nice woman who let us stay in her hotel.

She had a lot of other animals there, too!

I'd never seen animals who looked like this before.

They looked really funny!

But then they started to play tricks on me.

One of them took the Boss's wife's suitcase.

And another asked me to climb up some boxes.

Pretty soon, I ran into some big dogs. Big—and definitely <u>not</u> friendly.

In fact, they were downright mean.

And scary!

Even though he'd tried to hurt me, I gave the bull terrier my help when he needed it.

He sure did appreciate it. He even gave me his collar!

When I asked him why he had been mean in the first place, he said something about "a professional obligation to be malicious." I'm not sure what that means, but he's a nice dog now. If you treat someone nicely, they'll probably return the favor.

Unlike the Boss's farm, the city has a lot of animals that don't have homes.

These dogs were cold and hungry, so I took them back to the hotel.

And we gave them as much food as we could.

Then, out of the blue, my friend
Ferdinand appeared at the window!

For a while, everyone was having a nice time.
Until...

...all these humans stormed into the hotel! They weren't very nice.

They caught a lot of my friends and took them away.

But the rest of us weren't going to let that happen! We set out to find them.

I let my nose lead the way.

And we found them!

We snuck out very quietly. Everything was going really well. But then...

...we stumbled into a big, fancy banquet!

It didn't look as if the people there were too happy that we'd shown up.

BUt then the best thing happened. I found the Boss's wife!

A lot of people were making it difficult for the Boss's wife and me to leave the banqUet together.

Maybe they wanted to talk to us about living on a farm.

Or maybe they wanted to meet a sheep—pig.

The Boss's wife and I finally made it back to the farm, and we brought our new friends with us. They didn't have a home anymore. See, we rented out the hotel and used the money to save the farm!

We figured there was plenty of space on the farm for our new friends. And they sure did want to come back with us.

The Boss didn't mind, either. In fact, I think he was kind of happy. Once he tells me, "That'll do," I know everything is just fine!

I guess the trip to the Big City turned out to be a success after all!

Well, there you have it. Those are my favorite pictures from my most favorite adventures. But before you go, I just want to give you a big thank-you for looking at the pictures with me. It sure was nice. By the way, I think you're pretty nice, too! See ya!